CW01560774

Forgiveness

A Redwood Pack Novella

By
CARRIE ANN RYAN

Forgiveness copyright © 2013 Carrie Ann Ryan

All rights reserved.

ISBN-13: 978-1-943123-27-8

Cover Art by Charity Hendry

This book is a work of fiction. The names, characters, places, and incidents are products of the author's imagination or have been used fictitiously and are not to be construed as real. Any resemblance to persons, living or dead, actual events, locals or organizations is entirely coincidental. All rights reserved. With the exception of quotes used in reviews, this book may not be reproduced or used in whole or in part by any means existing without written permission from the author

Forgiveness

Adam Jamenson's courtship of his mate wasn't the most conventional. In fact, it didn't exist. Though he knows Bay loves him with every ounce of her soul, he needs to prove to her that he's worth it. Not only for her, but for himself. While they move on and learn to be the Enforcer mated pair, Bay will find herself on a path that leads her to a history beyond just her and Adam's mating. When she finds a locket rich in history and memories, she'll do all in her power to see those involved found and remembered. With Adam by her side, they'll both find the true meaning of forgiveness.

Author's Note: This is a novella set between books 4 and

5 to give you a taste of Bay and Adam. It is best that you have already immersed yourselves in the Redwood Pack world, however even new readers will enjoy a glimpse of one of the Redwood's favorite couples.

Dedication

To those who saw what was beneath the surface and knew my Enforcer had found his Redemption.

Acknowledgements

Thank you Lia Davis for not shaking your head at me when I said that Adam and Bay had more to tell us. They totally did.

Devon, without a doubt, I could not have done this without out. Thank you for your history advice and ability to see my characters for who they are.

Thank you Kelly and Fatin for all of your help with everything on the side. You know I can't do this on my own.

Finally, thank you Charity for bringing me out of the dark place when I need it. You know I'll always be there for you.

CHAPTER 1

She moved with grace, agility, and just that bit of sex appeal that had Adam Jamenson wishing they were alone, naked, sweaty, and doing every dirty thing that came to his mind. If one of the pups around his mate looked at her the way he was, Adam would have to beat the ever-loving crap out of him.

Twice.

FORGIVENESS

Bay Milton—no, Jamenson now, and, boy, did he like the sound of that—planted her feet in the cool grass and fisted her hands at her hips. Her wild, scarlet-red hair blew in the wind in a disarray of curls that reminded Adam of how she looked when she rode him long through the night, her hair bouncing along with those full breasts of hers.

He groaned and shifted his stance, careful not to wake a sleeping, snuggling Micah, who slept strapped into the harness on Adam's chest. Adam knew he must have looked like a completely different person from before, what with his son in a baby harness, the cane he hated using by his side, and his position on the sidelines, rather than in the thick of it.

Things had changed.

He had changed.

At least, he knew he had. He wasn't sure the rest of the Pack knew it yet. They still acted cautious around him, afraid to speak to him harshly or contradict him. That would change with time. He just had to show them that he had, in fact, changed.

"Okay, you guys, you're here because you're ready to find your positions in the Pack, but you don't know how to efficiently control your wolf —yet." Bay strode in front of the line of teens who had long since passed the age of their first change but still lacked the control and discipline needed to be an enforcer in the Redwood Pack.

Not *the* Enforcer. No, that was Adam's job.

One-legged and all.

His mate and love of his life, Bay, had turned out to be one fine Enforcer's mate, doing almost everything he had as the Enforcer, and because of their bond, she felt the same threats to the Pack that he did—just to a lesser extent.

It was as if the goddess knew the Redwoods—and Adam— needed another to step in when Adam was healing.

After all, having one's leg ripped off by a demon wasn't the easiest thing to get over.

If one ever did.

Nevertheless he would heal— he had to.

In fact, he'd already begun to because seeing his mate and child in the hands of the demon, Caym, had stolen any ounce of stubbornness and pride from him. He'd crawled, broken and bleeding, to the depths of any despair he'd thought he'd had and failed.

It had been Bay, his half-demon mate, who'd saved them all.

He watched her move gracefully again, this time showing the young wolves how to roll to duck a punch. Adam held back a groan as she stood up and wiggled her very sweet ass in snug yoga pants.

He didn't miss the quick glances of some of the older teens either.

Just for fun—and because, hell, he was the Enforcer—he let out a growl, marking what was his.

The young men froze, ducked their heads, and bared their throats. Maybe if he hadn't been sore as hell from standing on his new prosthetic leg for so long, he would have shown those boys exactly whom they were messing with, but he wasn't in the mood.

Plus, he had Micah attached to his chest, and that little one was more important than a pissing contest.

"Adam Jamenson," Bay scolded as she fisted her hands on her hips.

Adam smiled and watched her green eyes narrow and glow gold in annoyance. She was a feisty redhead—but *his* feisty redhead.

"What's wrong, darling?" he said causally, a grin threatening to break out over his face—something that was sure to scare the pups.

He heard a snicker or two from some of the pups who hadn't been watching his mate's ass, but they shut up quickly at her glare.

Then his mate rolled her eyes and tossed her hair behind her shoulders. "I swear boys never grow up, no matter how hard they try."

The girls in the group laughed at that, and Bay joined them.

Adam cleared his throat but didn't tug Bay close like he'd like to. He had to show that they were strong on their own as well as together while they were training. "That's a bit sexist, don't you think?" he teased.

Bay narrowed her eyes a bit more then winked. "Don't get me started on sexism in a werewolf Pack, oh mate of mine. I'll let you off the hook because you happen to be holding the cutest baby in the world."

Micah woke up at his mother's words and gurgled his appreciation. Adam lifted Micah a bit, patted his little diapered butt, and watched as Bay's face brightened. He knew his mate loved their child more than anything in the world, and he didn't fault her for it. No, he loved Micah just as much.

He hadn't always shown it.

He swallowed hard but didn't show any other expression at the memory. God, he'd been such an ass.

A fucking ass.

He'd walked away from his mate when she needed him the most because he'd had to say goodbye to Anna, his first mate who'd died so many years before. He'd walked away emotionally from Bay long before that.

Fuck, he needed to kick his own ass more than Caym had.

Adam was still surprised Bay had even stayed with him. Frankly, he wouldn't have blamed her for picking up Micah and walking away from him without a glance back.

Luckily for him, she'd stayed for Micah and the Pack.

He wasn't sure she'd stayed for him though—not that he deserved it.

He still needed to prove he'd changed. Prove he was worthy of her.

Though he didn't deserve it, he needed her forgiveness.

He watched as Bay finished up the training and sent the pups on their way. Ignoring the pain in his stump, he leaned on his cane to bend down and pick up the yoga mat she'd used to stretch out before the training. Images of just how she'd bent and twisted in order to do so made the pain in his leg worth it.

Because he was a wolf and not a normal human, his recovery time from the forced amputation was abundantly less than what it could have been. Already he could move without his cane if needed, and the prosthesis fit him perfectly. His brother and doctor,

North, refitted him every other day. Though Adam knew it was too frequent at this point, he let his brother worry about him only because it not only made Bay feel better but North and their mother as well.

He'd do anything to get the looks of fear off their faces. They'd tried to hide it, but he knew the fear was still there. He knew they were all afraid he'd fall into the abyss again and fracture, turning back into the wolf who drank too much, hurt those he loved, and continually threw his life away. He'd done that before he'd had his anchor—his Bay. And now, with Micah in the picture, he knew he had a future.

That is, as long as they defeated the Centrals.

That was another matter altogether.

"What do you think you're doing?" Bay asked as she took the mat from his hands.

Adam gave a small growl and frowned. "Helping you clean up."

Bay rolled her eyes. "I could have handled it. I don't want you to hurt yourself."

He watched as she winced at her words, but he shook his head before she could apologize. Even though it grated on him, he wasn't about to make an issue of it. He needed her to see him as more than a wounded man, but he also wanted her to need him more. She mattered more.

"I won't push myself. I promise. I just wanted to help my mate." He took her hand in his and brought it to his lips.

Her skin tasted of ice and berries, an intoxicating combination that set his wolf on edge, nudging at his skin. His wolf loved her and her wolf just as much as he did—something he loved about being a werewolf in the first place. There were two of them—two souls—sharing one body that loved and mated the same person and, in Bay's case, who also possessed two wolves.

"She's worth far more than either of us," his wolf said, leaning back to allow Adam the control he needed. It felt good to hear his wolf speak. It had been far too long since they'd shared a relationship where one wasn't afraid of the other—where one didn't blame the other for death and pain.

"Adam, you know I wasn't calling you weak," Bay said as she pulled back, running a hand over Micah's head.

Their son gurgled his delight, and she picked him up out of his harness, nuzzling his soft head against her chin.

Adam ignored her use of the word weak. He wasn't weak, not by a long shot. He was the damn Enforcer of the Redwood Pack—one legged and all.

The sight of his mate holding their child did odd things to Adam. All at once, he wanted to howl to the moon, praising the goddess for his virility as a father, and, at the same time, cover them with his body to ensure their safety.

Apparently, being a father caused one to go 'nucking futs'.

He grinned at the saying of one of the pups he'd taught.

Bay would hurt him if he kept cursing around Micah, and since his son was the smartest son of all sons, he knew Micah would pick up on the words soon.

After all, his Micah was the son of Bay, the most beautiful wolf in the world, and himself—a wolf not too bad if he listened to Bay.

"What is that smile for?" Bay asked as she started walking toward their home, Micah on her hip.

Adam took the mat from her arms and walked beside her, not using his cane as much as he had the previous week. The pain in his stump numbed as he got used to the walk.

"Just thinking about how our child is the smartest and best baby in the world."

Bay let out a laugh that sent shivers down his spine. "You're going to fill his little head with all that nonsense and he'll be one of those babies who pushes other babies around."

She kissed the top of Micah's head after she said it, and Micah let out a small laugh.

Soon their child would start talking and expressing his

thoughts. After all, their son was amazing.

"You're doing it again," Bay accused with a laugh in her voice. "You're doing that whole rooster thing where you thrust your chest out and show off your son, proving that your p-e-n-i-s can be wielded like the mightiest of swords."

"He's going to learn to spell that. And p-e-n-i-s isn't a dirty word."

She growled, and Micah let out a yelp. Quickly, she pulled him closer, and Adam took his turn to roll his eyes.

"Really? You're mothering him like he's the best baby in the world."

She glared at him over their son's head.

He winced, not because of her look of "doom", but because of the slight incline in their path.

"Only because you're the best mother in the world."

"Don't let your mother hear you say that," she said as they made their way into their home.

He looked over his shoulder, imagining his soft, yet Alpha, mother coming from behind and attacking him with a wooden spoon—or just her claws. "Don't say that. She could come at any moment."

"Your mother is the one all of us Jamenson women strive to be."

Adam frowned at her tone. "You're an amazing mother, Bay. You don't need to strive to be anyone but who you are."

She turned, rose to her toes, and kissed him softly. "Thank you for that. I was thinking more that if she could deal with the six of you boys and your sister, she can do anything."

Adam threw his head back and laughed. "True. My mother is one he—ck of a mother."

Bay glared at his almost-misstep and continued to the nursery. "I'm going to set him down for his n-a-p, and then we can snuggle." She winked as she said it, and his cock perked up.

Snuggle?

Hell yeah.

He cleared his throat. "I thought it was his dinner time." It wasn't as if he didn't want to snuggle with his mate—dear goddess how he wanted to do that—but they needed to care for Micah first.

Bay lifted a brow and smiled. "I'm going to feed, burp, and change him before his nap. It's the routine."

"Then let me help," Adam put in as he followed her to the nursery. It had once been a tomb of sorrow but now stood as a

17

testament of how much they loved their son.

"When you grow boobs, I'm sure you can," she teased as she sat down in the rocking chair and pulled down her yoga top.

All funny thoughts of him with boobs vanished at the sight of his mate's nipple before Micah attached himself like a greedy glutton.

The sight of his mate feeding their child was another one of those sights that threatened to bring him to his knees. Well, knee, since he had only one, but it was the principle of the matter.

He hobbled forward and leaned down to run a knuckle over the soft slope of her breast above their child's head.

"I love you, oh mate of mine," Bay whispered.

He looked into those green eyes that always ensnared him in the best ways possible. "I love you too." He kissed the top of his son's head then kissed the corner of Bay's mouth. "I'm going to start dinner so you're fed and well before we settle in. While it's cooking, I'll come back and change Micah for you so you can rest."

He needed to do everything he could for her. Words didn't matter. Lies were easily said, easily heard. Actions never lied— even if their intended purpose might be misconstrued.

His Bay had to know he cared for her and needed her in his life. He had to prove he was worth being in hers.

Bay tilted her head and reached out to stroke his cheek. "You don't need to do that. I can handle it."

Adam gave a small smile and pressed her palm to the side of his face, inhaling that sweet scent that brought him home while bringing him to the edge of sanity.

"Let me do this for you."

Let me do everything.

Bay let out a small sigh and jostled Micah. "Of course. I could use the rest."

He knew she was lying, even though she did indeed need to slow down. His Bay was trying to be the Enforcer by his side and learn how to be a new mother, all the while learning what it meant to be part of the Redwood Pack, rather than just a lone wolf.

They had all changed, and if Adam had anything to say about it, it would be for the better.

He walked to the kitchen, ignoring the pain in his stump, and started to make dinner, pulling out the chicken, vegetables, and rice. Though he was a red-meat type of guy—come on, he was a wolf after all—Bay loved eating healthy, so that's what they would do.

She had a sweet tooth he loved to indulge, meaning they went to Willow's Bakery or kitchen whenever they could to get the baked goods that made most want to orgasm on the spot. His brother Jasper, Willow's mate, was a lucky man.

Adam thought about his fierce Bay and smiled. He was pretty lucky as well.

As the chicken was cooking, he leaned against the counter, letting his body rest without the extra weight on his stump. He knew eventually he wouldn't even feel the pain. Though humans would always have to deal with it in some fashion, as a wolf, he would be able to lead a normal life, even if he had to learn to run on a prosthetic leg, so he could protect his family.

FORGIVENESS

As a wolf, he had only three legs, which might have scared some, but he took it as his due. His punishment. He could run with the best of them and fight for his family. Even so, he'd almost felt like he'd never be whole because he'd pushed his family away. It ached at him that he'd hurt them so much but he'd do whatever he could to fix it.

He deserved what he got because he'd hurt Bay so much.

He'd never forget the broken look on her face when he'd walked away—even if he'd only done it to say goodbye to his past. He should have stayed and explained. Instead, he'd broken his mate and almost destroyed their fragile mate bond.

He was the same man who'd beaten Jasper when his brother had threatened to walk away from Willow for her own safety during the beginning stage of their mating. Then, when Adam had thought he'd spend his life alone in penance for letting Anna and their unborn child die, Bay had come into his life, bringing Micah with her.

The grease from chicken popped in the pan, bringing him out of his thoughts. He quickly flipped it over before it burned, letting the smell of garlic and basil fill his nose.

"Micah's down for the count," Bay said as she walked into the kitchen and wrapped her arms around his middle from behind. Her sweet berry-and-ice scent settled over him, and he sighed.

"I thought I was going to do that for you so you could relax."

Bay moved to stand between him and the stove, meeting his eyes. "It was easy for me to do it. You can go in and kiss him later though. I know you love that little boy just as much as I do. You're

23

cooking dinner for us and doing everything else in the house you can these days. Take a breath, Adam. You're going to overwork yourself."

Didn't she see that he had to? Didn't she see that, if he didn't, he'd break because he needed to make sure she knew she and Micah were the best things in his life?

He took the chicken off the burner and turned off the heat before bringing Bay closer. "You're my everything, Bay Jamenson. I'm doing all of this because I can, because I don't want you to have to. You've done so much for me that I can't even breathe because I love you so much. Let me love you."

Bay smiled, her face brightening. "I will always let you do that, dork. You're my everything, just as much as I'm yours. Slow down with me.

Okay?" She ran her hands down his back, cupping his ass through his jeans. "What do you say we put the food in the fridge and make out like high school pups?"

Adam threw his head back and laughed. "Soon I'll be able to throw you over my shoulder and carry you to the bedroom. I'll show you just how much of a caveman I still am, but for now, your plan sounds like a great idea."

Bay's eyes darkened at his words, even as the thin rings of gold of her wolf's presence glowed around her irises. "You know what? I'm sure the food will be fine just waiting for us on the counter." She wiggled out of his hold and ran to the bedroom, shucking off her clothes as she did so.

Adam prowled behind her, stripping off his shirt. She'd have to help with his pants and leg, but she liked doing it, and he liked her hands on him.

His wolf growled in appreciation of what was to come, and he smiled.

Oh yes, this was one way to show how much he loved her.

His favorite way.

CHAPTER 2

"I'm pretty sure Micah is in heaven right now," Bay Jamenson teased as she watched her mother-in-law, Pat, rock Micah in her arms.

Melanie, her sister-in-law and Heir female, laughed. "Oh, yes, I totally agree. And just look at Finn watching. He knows it's his turn soon."

A pang hit Bay's heart before she could stop it. Finn was fine, really. He'd been so broken before that her body shook just watching the way the little boy, who used to smile and laugh so often, sat quietly on the floor waiting his turn for time with Grandma.

"He's doing okay, right?" Bay asked, unable to hold back the question.

Melanie's smile became strained, but she nodded. "Yes, he's just a different baby now." Her voice broke on the end, and she swallowed hard. "Sorry, I'm fine, really. It just hits me sometimes."

Bay wrapped an arm around the other woman's shoulders while they watched Pat play with their children. They'd come to Pat's house so the Alpha female could indulge in babies while Bay and Melanie helped clean out the attic—something that hadn't been done in decades. Apparently the elders had just thrown things up there, and Pat had let it happen so everyone would be happy. Well, now the Alpha female wanted her space back, so the Jamenson women were going to help her without being asked. They all loved Pat like their own mothers and would do anything for her—even dig through dusty boxes so she wouldn't have to.

Bay just prayed that her psychometry—her ability to see memories from touching certain objects—didn't flare up. It was most likely going to happen anyway, but hopefully, it would be good memories that didn't wear her out.

Mel sniffed then shook her head. "Okay, let's get to work so I can get my mind off things that make me want to snatch Finn up and never let him go."

Bay smiled, thinking in the same circumstances, she'd want to do the same to Micah at any given moment. "Sounds like a plan. Pat, we're going up to the attic. If we don't come out in a couple hours, the boxes ate us."

Pat raised a brow and settled Micah against her shoulder as Finn quietly climbed to sit next to her. Again, that slight pain sliced through her at the sight of the now solemn little boy who used to smile with the greatest of ease.

"If you're afraid of a little dust, I have no hope for you," Pat teased, and Bay stuck out her tongue like the tough Enforcer mate she was.

Finn cracked a small smile, and Melanie squeezed her hand. Bay would totally act like a silly pup any day of the week to see that little boy smile again.

Micah grinned in his little baby way, and Bay's heart melted.

She'd never thought she'd be a mom—there hadn't been options when she'd hidden most of her life from the other wolves. Now that she did have her own son, though, she wouldn't change it for the world.

And she had a feeling that, one day, she'd have even more babies crawling around the house. She knew Adam wanted more, even if he didn't say as much. Her mate had lost his first child all those years ago, along with Anna, his first mate, and it had scared him out of living life to the fullest. Now, though, he was moving on and becoming the man she knew he could be—one that she loved with the fullness of her heart.

She couldn't wait to see him hold more babies and melt in that special way the strong warrior in him tended to do.

FORGIVENESS

Melanie elbowed her in the side, and Bay shook herself out of her thoughts. "Sorry, I was woolgathering. I'm not afraid of a little dust, but from what you've told us about the attic, I don't think little will be an adequate word to describe it."

Melanie snorted beside her, and Bay rolled her eyes.

Pat narrowed hers, though Bay could see the laughter rolling in them. "You know, I could be doing this on my own. You don't have to help."

Bay let out a playful growl. "No, you get to sit down and play with some of your grandbabies. If you're really lucky, Willow and Hannah will stop by with those kiddos of theirs and you can swim in baby love. Melanie and I can handle it; you do too much for us already."

Pat sighed and pulled both boys closer. "Sometimes I feel like it's not enough."

Bay walked toward her Alpha female and knelt. "You're keeping us strong. Never forget that."

Melanie knelt beside her and rubbed a hand over Finn's knee. He didn't giggle like he used to, but he kept the smile on his face—progress.

Pat let out a breath and shook her head. "Get going, you two. I can handle these boys. We've enough melancholy in our lives without bringing it into every conversation."

Bay and Melanie left Pat to her grandbabies and headed up to the attic.

"Ready for this?" Melanie asked, a smile on her face, a joyous welcome over the stoic emotions that her Heir female had shown recently.

Bay opened the door and froze, a curse escaping from the tight line of her lips. "Well then."

Mounds of boxes covered every corner and most places in between. Dust, as well as more than a few cobwebs, covered every inch. Old sheets lay over some furniture, or at least that's what Bay thought the shapes were. Newspapers lay in stacks on the floor, yellowed with age and neglect.

This was not the attic of Pat Jamenson, who was usually so tidy and organized in her homely nature.

No, this was a hoarder's haven.

A heap of dust and memories that made Bay's hands burn.

"Well, hell," Melanie muttered under her breath. "This is going to take days, if not weeks."

"True, but it's not like we have to do it all at once."

Mel nodded and started walking around, lifting a few corners of boxes, coughing as the dust rose in the air. Bay envied the way Mel could walk around and touch tokens from the past with such ease. Bay couldn't control her powers that had scared her all her life.

Though she'd never heard of another wolf who could glean memories from the surface of items that held intense and sometimes painful memories, she hoped to the goddess that it had come from her mother's people...and not her father's.

She was half-demon after all and she didn't want to think about the so called heritage that came with that.

Bay shook her head, clearing out those thoughts that would lead to no good. She already

35

worried enough for two people that the blood that also ran through her son's veins would harm him, but she couldn't think about that now.

No, now she had to worry about cleaning, something that Pat hadn't had time to do for decades because this hadn't been her mess.

"Bay? You sure you're going to be okay? Can't you wear gloves or something?" Mel had sat down in front of a few boxes and started opening them, making piles, using an organizational system that Bay only dreamed of having.

"Gloves don't really work. I mean, the skin contact is what brings about the more intense memories, but when I wear gloves, I sometimes get the residual memories and they last longer, almost like a stale taste on my tongue."

She couldn't quite explain it to someone who had never felt the power of another's memories or the ability to control her wolf with an ease that rivaled an Alpha's. Bay was different— something that she'd tried to hide her whole life, only to find comfort in her Enforcer's arms.

"I'll never get over all the powers some of you have," Mel said as she gingerly picked up a piece of metal that Bay couldn't quite identify. Mel put it in what had to be the trash pile and continued. "I have the ability to feel the Pack somewhat through Kade, and as time moves on, that connection is getting stronger. I think the goddess knew I needed time to wrap my head around it all."

Mel had been the most analytical of them all, not fully believing in wolves and the things that went bump in the night. But fate had brought her here, and now Mel was growing more comfortable with her newfound wolf half. Her Heir female had been through the change by force, not by birth. Melanie had been purposely almost ripped to shreds by Edward, the Alpha, so she could be a wolf. Only being near death and the bite of a wolf could bring on the change— something they all wished was different. If Melanie could last through that, she could last through anything.

"You're rocking it now," she finally said. "Now, let's getting digging." Bay sat near Mel and opened another box, hoping she wouldn't relive memoires.

Her hand wrapped around an old lamp, and she sighed as nothing came.

She and Mel worked for another hour, chatting about what they uncovered and the goings on within the Pack. It was nice to have someone to share things with. She knew that any one of the Jamensons would talk to her about most things—even the unmated ones like Maddox, North, and Cailin.

They really were a family—something she treasured.

"So, how's Adam?" Mel asked, her voice a little too casual.

Bay resisted the urge to growl. The entire family walked on eggshells around the man she loved, even though they treated him like the family he was.

"Fine."

Melanie sighed and put down an antique phone she'd been looking at. "You know we worry, Bay. We can't help it."

"Worry about what? That he'll run off again? Or that he's less of a man because of what happened to him?"

Melanie growled, the strength of her wolf surprising Bay. It shouldn't have, considering her ranking in the Pack. "No, not at all. In fact, we all welcome the fact that Adam is different. He doesn't think we know, but we do. Even though I'd known him only a short time during his grief, I knew he needed to move on. Yes, it sounds callous, but he was killing himself."

"He's better now." It was the truth. Her Adam wasn't the same man she'd met in the bar and mated with, only to be left behind when he'd ignored the bond.

"Yes, he isn't grieving the way he was. And no, we don't look at him as any less of an Enforcer because he doesn't have a leg. Think better of us." Mel's eyes narrowed, and Bay growled.

"Really? Then why are you still acting differently around

him? He's doing his best to prove he's worth something, and you guys aren't treating him like you should."

"That's not why, Bay. It's because of you." Mel's shoulders sank, and Bay blinked.

"Me? What do I have to do with it?"

"Bay, Adam hurt you in the worst way possible. Even though he's our brother—yes, he's my brother though we don't share blood—he was the one who pushed you away and made you hurt. It's hard to forgive someone for that."

Bay closed her eyes, suppressing the emotions warring within her. "I know you guys are trying to help. Believe me, I'm touched and thankful in all ways possible that you guys love me enough to fight for me, but there's nothing to forgive."

"Really? Nothing?"

"*Nothing*. I know why he did it, and frankly, if I hadn't gotten over it, we would never have been able to move on. I want a future, Mel, not a past to reflect on and worry over."

Mel scooted over and wrapped her arm around Bay's shoulders. "And when we keep harping on it, it's only hurting you and Adam more. I guess I should have been more perceptive on that, right? I'm still getting the hang of this whole Heir thing."

Bay leaned her head against Mel's. "You're not too shabby at it, hon. And, honestly, if Adam hadn't already been torturing himself over it, it wouldn't be an issue."

"What do you mean?"

"He's doing so much to prove he's changed from the man who turned his back to grieve. He's practically laying himself prostrate at my feet to earn a forgiveness that he should know he already has. He doesn't need to say he's sorry—though he's done that. His apology and grief for hurting me is in every action and every breath he takes."

Bay took a breath, willing her emotions to cool. She couldn't cry or scream now, not when she needed to voice her concerns to someone who would listen and do all in her power to help.

"He doesn't need to prove he's changed," Bay continued. "I know he's different. I know he's the man I love. I don't need to forgive him because I forgave him long ago when he sacrificed himself for me. Yes, he was an ass, but he was my ass. My mate. I didn't have the easiest mating, but so what? I get to have a family—something I didn't have before."

Mel nodded. "I know, hon."

"He doesn't need my forgiveness. But I just wish he'd forgive himself."

"Have you told him that?" Mel asked gently.

"I think," Bay mumbled. "I've tried, but I don't think he wants to listen. He's doing all in his power to prove he's worthy of me, but he's always been, even if he hadn't shown it."

"Then tell him, Bay."

Bay nodded. "I guess he's not going to know if I don't really say what's on my mind."

Mel's eyes danced with laughter. "I think that's the thing with most men and women. They need to be told."

Bay laughed, her worries just that much lighter. "True. At least I'm not alone in that. Now let's stop wallowing in my issues and get back to work."

Mel huffed out a breath. "I know some people would just

throw the whole lot out, but I can't do that."

Bay nodded in full agreement. "People saved this for a reason. The main reason might have been the inability to throw away crap, but there have to be a few things in here that can be used or showcased in the den center so people can have a look at history."

Mel's eyes brightened. "That's exactly what I've been thinking. We can make lists and organize by year and everything."

Bay held back a groan. "Sometimes I forget that you were once a chemist with OCD."

Her sister-in-law grinned. "Oh, I never forget. I know lists and things aren't your thing. I think Cailin would want to help since she likes putting things in their place."

"Mostly her brothers," Bay teased and laughed right along with Mel.

They continued to go through things, mostly finding junk with the occasional item to be re-evaluated later. It was nice to do something that had nothing to do with war or training. Though she wanted to look toward the future with Adam and Micah, she never wanted to forget the past that could help them learn how to function in the future. Before the Jamensons, she hadn't had a family or any chance to know of her own past, so it was nice to look at another's.

Bay reached into the almost empty box and wrapped her palm around a locket, immediately wishing she hadn't.

Images of a young woman with tears running down her face mixed with an image of that same woman running through a field

46

into the arms of a young man. Bay couldn't discern their faces or even their clothes. She could only feel the love between them as it faded to a deep agony that threatened to steal her breath.

Flashes of pain, sorrow, and lost hope slapped at her, causing her to clutch her chest with her free hand as she tried to pull herself out of the vision.

"Bay!" Melanie called, and Bay felt the other woman pull her into her arms.

Bay closed her eyes tightly as bile rose in her throat, the vision leaving her as quickly as it came, leaving her shaken and her palms clammy.

"That was a vision, right? What can I do?"

Thankful Melanie hadn't asked what she'd seen, considering she wouldn't be able to formulate words anyway, Bay nodded.

"Okay, let's get you downstairs and to Pat. I think you need to rest and drink some water. We've done enough anyway."

Though fear laced Melanie's tone, the strong command just reminded Bay that the other woman was truly the Heir's mate and could handle anything in her path.

Bay stood on shaky legs, her hand still clasped around the locket, the image fading away. She might see another image later, or the same one, or never again. She just didn't know. What she'd seen might have overwhelmed her, but she wasn't going to forget it any time soon. There had to be a reason she'd have a vision with this particular piece. When she'd had time to calm down and go through it with Adam, she'd be able to decide what to do.

"What on earth happened?" Pat asked as she hurried toward them.

"She had a vision when she touched the locket," Mel explained as she sat Bay on the couch. "I'm going to call Adam and get her some water."

Pat nodded, and Mel ran toward the kitchen. Her mother-in-law knelt before her and cupped her cheeks.

"Did it hurt? What can I do for you? You don't need to worry about Micah. He and Finn are down for naps in the grandbaby room."

Relief spread through her, even though she hadn't known she'd been worried that she couldn't see her son. Sometimes a mother's irrational fear needed soothing more than pain.

"I'm fine, really," Bay said, her voice scratchy. "It just surprised me. That's all."

49

Pat looked at her hard then nodded.

"Adam's on his way. Apparently he felt something flare through the mate bond and was on his way anyway." Mel handed Bay a glass of water, and she drained it in one large swig.

"Good. You're both done for the day," Pat ordered. "I want you to go home and rest, Bay. If you feel you need to share what you've seen, I'm here. Just as I know the rest of us are for you, dear. I know your gift is personal, so I'm not going to make you tell me anything. I know my son will take care of you."

Bay nodded, her eyes filling with tears. That had been the exact thing to say. She'd needed to hear that the family trusted her mate to care for her. Bay believed it. She only needed Adam and the family to do the same.

50

"Bay!" Adam called as he scrambled in, his cane nowhere to be seen.

"I'm here, Adam. Everything's okay."

Ignoring her words, he rushed toward her as Pat moved out of the way quickly. He ran his hands down her arms as he sat in front of her, careless of his new leg.

"Melanie told me what happened, but I need to hear that you're safe," he whispered, his words sliding over her like a caress.

"I'm fine, Adam. You know how visions take it out of me."

Adam nodded but kept running his hands over her as if to prove she was really there.

"I'm taking you home and putting you in bed. You don't have to worry about a thing."

She cupped his bristled cheek and pulled him closer, rubbing

51

her lips against his. "I'm not worried. I have you."

She pulled back as his eyes glowed. God, she loved this man.

"Do you need me to steady you?" he asked. He was strong enough to carry her, she knew he didn't want to risk dropping her and show weakness—let alone hurt her.

"I'll be fine. Can you get Micah?"

Adam nodded and walked to the back room. She'd shown that she trusted Adam to hold and care for their son like she'd been doing before. That had to be enough.

"Thank you," she said to the two women who stared at her with worry.

"You're welcome," Melanie said. "I know Adam will take care of you, so I'm not too worried. If you want to talk about what you saw, you need only to call."

Adam came back into the room, carrying a sleeping Micah in his arms, and she stood on unsteady legs to follow him out after they said their goodbyes. It was a short walk to their home, and Bay let Adam put Micah down in his crib as she walked to their bedroom.

She tugged off her jeans and shirt then did the same to her bra and panties. She didn't have the energy to make love, but she wanted to feel free.

Adam growled behind her, his appreciation evident as she got into bed. He pulled the covers over her and kissed her softly.

"I'm glad you're okay, Bay," he whispered.

"Hold me?" she asked, needing his touch. Her wolf nudged against her, needing the same contact.

"Anything," he answered and stripped to his skin.

FORGIVENESS

She ran her gaze along his honeyed skin, loving the way his muscles gleamed with each movement. Later she'd run her tongue along his tattoo because she wanted to and because he loved it.

Carefully, he sat at the edge of the bed, removed his prosthesis, climbed into bed, and brought her back to his front, spooning her. Though she felt his erection hard and full along her skin, they both ignored it, needing touch and warmth rather than release.

"I love you," he whispered. "We'll deal with whatever you saw when you're ready."

Bay closed her eyes, his heat settling her. "I know. You're the one I want by my side no matter what. I love you as well."

Later, they'd worry about what she'd seen and what must be done about it. She knew this one was different from the others, as if the goddess herself was telling her to look into the locket's past. For now she'd rest in his arms and block out the world. He was her mate, her love, and her life. At the moment, she didn't need any more than that.

CHAPTER 3

Bay woke to roaming hands, touching, caressing, and heat. Adam traced her belly with his fingertips then slid down to her sex, teasing her clit and slowly entering her one finger at a time. Her mate was going to kill her in anticipation, no doubt about it. She moaned and wiggled her ass so she rocked into his cock, needing him in her more than anything in the world.

They rarely had time together in the mornings anymore, not with Micah and their duties overshadowing everything else in their lives. The war loomed closer, taking more of their lives than ever, but right now, she didn't want to care about that. She didn't want to care about Caym, the war, the locket, or anything else. As Adam rubbed his thumb along her clit, pressing harder as she panted, she knew this morning would be different, and they'd take the time for themselves.

Finally.

"Adam," she whispered as he ran his hand up her stomach, cupping her breast. Her nipple pebbled against his palm, and she felt him shudder behind her, his strong body framing her, the heat of it like a furnace on a cold winter's night.

"Good morning, mate of mine," he whispered into her ear, his low voice sending shivers straight to her womb. He nibbled on her ear lobe, a gentle touch of teeth on flesh that almost made her come right there.

"I guess..." She gasped as he lifted her leg and slowly, oh so slowly, slid into her, filling her up until she was so full she could barely breathe, barely think. "...we should get up for the day."

"I'm already up, my Bay. Now stop thinking and feel."

He ran his hands down her body, holding her close as he pumped into her from behind, his cock sliding in and out of her slick channel, bringing her closer to the edge as she panted for him.

Her Adam pulled out fully then slid in and out in short quick bursts before slamming home, sending her over her peak. She shuddered, her body flushing, heating, and spiraling as she came. Her wolf howled, clawing to the surface in search of her mate, needing to be just as close, just as loved.

"Bay," he groaned as he came with her, his seed filling her to the brim.

Hannah, their Healer, had given her herbs as birth control, so there would be no baby yet—but soon. Hopefully.

"I love filling you up with my cum. I can't wait to fill you up so full that we make another baby. I didn't get to watch you with Micah, but I'll watch this."

Her heart filled and broke at the same time. Yes, Adam had missed much of her pregnancy with Micah, but that would be different with the next one. The fact that he knew that and wanted to make a change just showed her how much he'd grown. The fact that she wanted to be with him and not a lone wolf showed her how much *she'd* grown.

"I know you will, Adam. You're already an amazing father," she added, needing to make sure he understood.

His grip on her hips tightened for just a bit before he relaxed, placing a soft kiss on her neck then grazing his teeth along the mate mark. "I'm trying, Bay. Trying hard."

"You're doing everything right. Don't forget that."

"I love you, Bay."

"Love you too, Adam. Now let's get up and get ready for our day, or I'll end up staying in bed with you and never leaving."

Adam rolled his hips, his still hard cock touching her in that spot she loved. "I could do this for hours, days, years." At his words, he pulled out of her, and she immediately felt the loss. "But we do need to get going. We have a few things to do before the hunt tonight."

Bay rolled off the bed and walked to bathroom as Adam fit his leg. He didn't like her watching him do it, so she let him be. She'd do everything else to make sure he knew she found him sexy.

"I love our hunts. I never got to do them as a lone wolf. It's so different now. I love the way we all run together and let our wolves roam within the den— even with the Centrals around."

She jumped in the shower and stepped under the spray as she heard Adam walk in, still naked but his prosthesis on.

"I'm glad you're enjoying them. Kade thinks Finn's about ready to change, so soon we'll have a pup with us."

Bay smiled at the thought of a little baby pup roaming with them. Melanie and Kade would be protective of their son, but Finn would love the hunt, much like herself.

"I'd get in the shower with you, but I hear Micah moving around," Adam said, his voice holding a bit of pain that worried her.

"What's wrong?"

He cracked open the shower door and smiled. God, she loved those jade-green eyes. "I'm fine. I just hate showing off my three legs when we run as wolves. I know you don't care, and neither does my family, but it's still odd."

She moved forward and framed his face. "Oh, baby, I'm sorry. I didn't even think about that."

He kissed her softly. "It's not that big a deal. I'll get over it." He reached around and smacked her ass, sending a sharp sting of pleasure, rather than pain. "I like the way your eyes darken when I do that. I'll have to make sure I do it more often."

She whimpered, her wolf just as needy as her, even more so now with the full moon coming, and her wolf was already on edge.

"Adam..."

"No, I'm leaving to go feed our son some oatmeal. Then you can do the rest while I shower. I have a few things to do with Jasper for Larissa and Neil, and then we can go on our hunt."

"Larissa and Neil are Kade and Melanie's friends, right?"

Adam nodded and pulled on some sweats as she washed out her hair. "Yeah. Mel knew Larissa from her old job, and they asked Jasper to help with an add-on to their home since they don't want the kids to have to share a room anymore."

"So you're going to help Jasper build?" Even though she was worried about the pressure on his leg, she smiled at the thought of him working so cohesively with the Pack.

"Yep. I'm not as good as Jasper or Kade, but I like to help when I can."

"Then you'll be all nice and sweaty before we roam as wolves and find ourselves naked in the forest," she teased.

Adam groaned and shook his head. "You know I can't very well swing a hammer with a hard-on."

Bay laughed and rubbed her loofa over her breasts, loving the way Adam's eyes glowed gold, his gaze following the soap suds.

"I know there's a dirty hammer joke in there somewhere, but I'm a little too turned on to think about it."

Adam closed the shower door with a *click*. "Enough, you. We have things to do, and yet, all I want to do is press your tits up against the shower door and fuck you hard."

"Well hell," she mumbled, her breasts feeling heavy, aching.

"You deserve that, mate of mine," Adam said with a chuckle as he left her alone in the shower.

Oh hell, it was going to be a long day.

After Adam had left and Micah had been dropped off at Cailin's so her sister-in-law could bond with her nephew, Bay felt out of sorts. She could have gone to help the Enforcers, the wolves who worked under Adam, but she wasn't needed there today. She also could have gone to Pat and Edward's to work in the attic, but she didn't feel up to it yet.

Yes, the moon's pull made it feel as though her skin was too tight, and she needed a run, but that would come later.

FORGIVENESS

Now, though, she needed to look into the locket and try to find out what she could do about it. She hadn't had time to talk to Adam about it yet, and she knew, though he wanted to know what was going on, he wasn't going to push her, not anymore. It was just another way she knew their relationship had grown over time.

Bay stood on her porch, the slight breeze whipping her hair around, and let out a breath. Even with all that was going on around her with the war, she only had thoughts for her family...and that locket. The vision had shaken her more so than others— even when she'd seen Anna and Adam together when she'd touched the mantel all those months ago. She knew she wouldn't be able to focus on anything else, not really, until she solved the mystery of the locket.

What she wasn't, however, was a sleuth. Meaning she'd need help. There was only one person she knew who could help her with the history of the Pack—Reed, her brother-in-law. Though he wasn't a true historian, he did meet with the elders regularly to go through an oral history of the Pack. Then he'd write it down or paint it, depending on how it needed to be done. Considering the way old wolves lived, sometimes they forgot to document their past beyond a mere memory, but Reed was helping with that.

Determined, she headed off to Reed's, knowing he'd probably be home since he had one-month-old twins at home. She smiled at the thought of little Kaylee and Conner. Hannah and North had been the only two people who'd known of the twins, so it had been a shock for Reed and Josh, Hannah's mates, during the delivery.

Apparently they'd both fallen on their asses while Hannah lay on the delivery table. Bay would have paid good money to see that.

Bay knocked on the door quietly, knowing they'd hear her since they were wolves, but she also didn't want to wake the babies in case they were asleep. Josh answered the door, wearing only unbuttoned jeans, his hair in disarray. Even though Bay was happily mated, that didn't mean she couldn't look her fill. After all, Josh was one sexy, built man with spiral tattoos running down his arms from the demon bite that had changed him.

"Hey," he croaked then rubbed his face. "Come on in. Did we know you were coming?"

Bay shook her head and walked into the living room,

which looked as if a bomb of baby items had blown up.

She turned and raised a brow. "Why haven't you called the family for help?" she asked, not caring if she was breaking a rule or something.

Josh just smiled, making him look younger. "We're handling it okay. There *are* three of us and only two of them."

Bay laughed. "There's only me and Adam, and yet Micah seems to cause us to make as much of a mess. Remember Mel and Kade when they first had Finn? They had to take a break and leave the den for a bit. All babies run us down, but we have a family we can rely on."

Just saying those words made her feel giddy. It hadn't been that long ago that she had no one, and now she had everything she could want.

"Pat and Edward get grandparent time tomorrow," Hannah said as she walked in, her body still full from her recent pregnancy but beautiful.

"Are the babies asleep?" Bay asked after she hugged her sister-in-law.

"Finally. I think I'm going to go pass out now," Hannah said on a laugh.

Josh pulled his mate into his arms and kissed her forehead. "Go to bed, baby. We'll take care of everything else."

"No, I'm fine, really."

Bay smiled at the way Josh took care of Hannah, even though she knew Hannah took care of her men just the same.

"I thought I heard a visitor," Reed said as he walked into the room in a paint-stained T-shirt and jeans. "What's up, Bay?"

"I know you're all super busy, but I wanted to see if I could borrow Reed for a bit," she answered, immediately feeling bad for even thinking about taking him away from his family for a minute.

Hannah raised a brow. If she'd been a wolf, Bay was sure the other woman would growl. One did not mess with another's mates—especially one who was in the middle of a hormonal craze. Even though they were family, sometimes the wolf took over.

Bay just shook her head and laughed. "I need his help with some history. That's it."

Hannah smiled, and Bay laughed again. Yes, she loved the Jamensons totally.

"What can I help you with, Bay?" Reed asked as he walked toward her, pulling her in for a hug. They were wolves, after all, and loved—no, needed—touch.

"It's just a history thing," she said. She hadn't told Adam about

71

the locket yet, and now she felt bad that she was here letting the others know.

Hannah and Josh seemed to understand and left the room, presumably to go rest or see to the babies.

Reed gestured toward the couch, and Bay went to sit down, pushing a stack of nappies and blankets out of the way as she did so.

Reed blushed at the mess, and Bay just sighed. "It's okay that your house looks like it does, you know. You're new parents with twins."

"Twins we didn't know about, so we couldn't prepare our lives," Reed said wryly.

"Well, Hannah knew, so she was ready."

Reed just rolled his eyes and rested his head against the couch. "Don't let me fall asleep on you, okay?"

"Sure thing."

"Now, what was it you wanted to talk about, and why is it so secret? And, yes, I can tell it's secret from the way you're acting."

Bay blushed, awkwardness taking over. "It's not that it's a secret. It's more that I haven't had the chance to tell Adam about it yet."

Reed nodded, seeming to understand. "And you don't want to hurt his feelings by telling everyone else first."

"Right in one," she said, grateful she had such a loving family.

"So?"

She pulled the locket out of her pocket, relief filling her that she didn't get another vision from it when she touched it.

"Nice," Reed said as he gently took it from her. "What's it about?"

"I have no idea. I found it in your parents' attic, so it probably belongs to an elder since that's where most of that stuff came from, but when I touched it the first time, I got a vision."

Reed nodded. "That's what Kade said after he talked to Mel."

Bay rolled her eyes. Trust the Jamensons to have the grapevine down pat. "Well, yes. The thing is, I couldn't really figure out what it was telling me." She explained what she'd seen, and Reed frowned.

"It sounds like it needs to find its owner."

Bay nodded, relieved. "Exactly, but I have no idea how to do that. I didn't recognize who it was, but that means nothing."

"Well, I don't recognize the locket, so I won't be much help, but you can talk to the elders. They might know. Or you might get lucky and find its owner among them."

"What if it hurts them? Not physically, but emotionally."

"If you're not sure, then you don't have to share it. It's gone all these years being lost. It doesn't have to be found now."

Bay shook her head. "No, I found it, so I can't just bury it away."

Reed smiled. "I figured. If you want, I can tell the elders tomorrow that you'll be stopping by at some point so they're ready. They're not fans of surprises."

"Don't tell them about the locket though. I think I need to be the one to do that, even if it's a surprise."

"No problem."

Bay left after saying her goodbyes, a sense of purpose filling her. She'd find out who had owned that locket and put the matter to rest. Even though the locket wasn't hers, and really had nothing to do with her, she wanted to make sure it found its peace. It had called to her for a reason, and she wasn't going to ignore it. Bay had felt the pain in the locket calling out to her, needing closure, and she wouldn't let it, or its owner, down.

CHAPTER 4

The smell of the forest seeped into Adam's senses, and he took a deep breath, inhaling the sweet scent of ice and berries from the very delectable woman by his side. He wrapped an arm around Bay's shoulders, and she snuggled deep, making his wolf howl to be let out so he could play.

FORGIVENESS

They stood in their backyard, rather than in the circle with the rest of the Pack. He knew it was stupid, but he'd rather change in front of Bay alone than meet the others to do it. His family seemed to understand, even if he knew they wished it were different.

He had issues getting his prosthesis off and changing, so he usually had to kneel awkwardly to shift into his wolf. It didn't bother him as much as it had, but he wasn't quite ready to show off his stump to the Pack.

"Are you ready for the hunt?" Bay asked as she ran a hand up and down her arm.

Their wolves were riding each of them hard as the moon pulled at their bodies. They'd have to change quickly so they got some relief from the ache. Usually they could deal with the moon and not change, but it had been too long for either of them.

"Past ready," he grunted.

Bay threw her head back and laughed. "Is it bad that I'm really happy that the non-wolves are taking care of all the kids tonight?"

Although, as werewolves, they didn't have to go on the hunt when the moon called, lately in the wake of the war with the Centrals, they'd decided to let their wolves run free. The tension and loss rode their wolves hard, and they needed this. In contrast, though the witches and humans, and demons in Josh's case, liked going on hunts with them, there were too many young children around who needed to be watched.

Soon those kids would grow up and shift on their own, but for now Hannah, Josh, Larissa—their friend and another witch like Hannah—and a few other mates would be in the town center with the children who couldn't shift yet.

"No," he finally answered. "It's not bad at all. We need to let our wolves roam and, at the same time, know our son is safe and warm. Eventually he'll shift and hunt with us."

Bay's face brightened, her green eyes going wide. "Oh, he's going to be such a cute little pup. I can't wait to see what color his fur is when he shifts."

Though the color of wolves' fur didn't always match their hair color, it was subtly hereditary. Micah wouldn't be a white-coated pup because neither he nor Bay was, but Micah could be anything else.

"He's already the best baby there ever could be," Adam said, echoing his statement from before.

Bay rolled her eyes and pulled back from him. "What did I say about spoiling him?"

Adam tilted his head. "Do it often?"

His mate snorted and proceeded to strip out of her clothing so they could shift. Adam's gaze landed on her full breasts and her rose-colored nipples that seemed to be begging for his touch.

His cock filled, and he groaned.

"Oh, no you don't. We need to shift. Then we can hump like bunnies." Bay's ass wiggled as she pulled off her pants. Then she turned around so she could bend over to take off her panties.

"Fuck."

If a man could die from a hard-on, he'd be one of them.

Still bent over, she wiggled again, this time giving him a full-on view of that pussy he loved to taste then pound into.

"What?" she asked, her tone overly innocent.

"Just fuck," he grumbled and sat down on the ground to strip and take off his leg. It was awkward as hell, especially with his dick bouncing against his stomach, but he needed to shift so they could hunt.

Then he could fuck his mate into oblivion.

As she shifted into her wolf, Adam growled and let the pain wash over him. His bones broke and realigned, his muscles stretched and moved, conforming to his new body. Soon, he stood on three legs, his wolf taking over, ready to hunt, ready to feel.

He threw back his head and howled, Bay following him in harmony, the sounds of wildness and mating.

This is what he'd been missing.

They ran together as wolves, letting their animals rise to the surface and control them more than when they were in their human forms. Soon they found themselves surrounded by his family, the array of color and scents almost overwhelming, but it didn't matter.

They were his family.

With Bay by his side, his home.

His Alpha and father howled to the moon goddess, and the rest of them followed suit, letting go of their pain and sorrow, if only for the night.

Soon, they were on the run, chasing each other or a sign of prey; it didn't matter. They just ran because they wanted to, because they *had* to.

After an hour of running, their wolves leading them, Adam

stopped in a stand of trees and waited for Bay. He'd run faster than he'd had to because he'd wanted to prove himself, though he hadn't needed to.

He was better than he'd thought, his stump not hurting with his hard run. He was an alpha male and needed to get over himself—not something easily done.

As soon as his mate came to his side, he shifted back, the pain just as intense as it had been turning into a wolf.

He lay on the ground afterward, panting, his body slick with sweat. Soon Bay came to his side, also in human form and pressed a kiss to his lips. He greedily licked and sucked, wanting more of her.

She pulled back, her eyes still gold from her wolf, her hair wild around her face. "Why did you shift back?" she asked, even as she ran a hand down his stomach then lower to grip his dick.

Adam groaned and pumped his hips, wanting her touch. "I want to feel your body wrapped around mine under the moonlight, my Bay."

She smiled and released him. "I like that idea. We could have done it at home though. That way you wouldn't have to shift back."

Though most could have walked back naked to their homes, Adam wouldn't be able to with only one leg. He'd have to shift back to his wolf form to make it home, but it didn't matter.

"I don't care. I want my mate, and I want to show you how much I do. So let me love you." He cupped her breast, letting the heavy weight fill his palm. She moaned and leaned into him before moving back. "Why do you keep moving away from me?"

"Because I want to make sure we're alone," she said as she looked over her shoulder.

Adam laughed. "Don't worry. We can hear them if they get closer. Plus, I'm pretty sure all the mated pairs are out doing exactly what we're about to do. So hop on, mate of mine."

Bay giggled. Giggled.

God, he loved when she let go of everything and just acted like a woman in love. Hell, he loved when he let go of everything and acted like a man in love.

Their wolves were still riding them, the wildness almost overwhelming. There would be time later for slow and sensual. Today, this time, was about hard, fast, and being together, just the two of them.

Bay grinned and straddled him. He ran his hands up her sides, loving the way her soft skin beckoned him. He cupped her breasts, and she leaned closer, throwing her head back as she rocked that wet pussy of hers against his rock-hard cock. He molded her breasts to his hands as he arched his hips, wanting to have her take him.

"Bay," he whispered, his voice hoarse as he tried to gain control.

She moved to look at him, their gazes locking. Then she moved up, letting her pussy rub along the head of his dick.

"Slide down, baby," he grunted. "If you don't, I'm going to ram up and take control."

She smiled coyly. "Oh, no you don't. This one's mine." She rolled her hips like a belly dancer then slid down his length until she sat on his hips, his cock surrounded by her tight, oh-so-warm heat.

"Hell," he said, and she laughed.

"Hell indeed. God, I love when you fill me."

"Good thing because I'm going to keep filling you until the end of our days."

She pressed her palms to his shoulders, giving herself an anchor, then proceeded to move up and down his cock, rolling her hips as she did so. They set a fast rhythm, their wolves rising to the surface as their breaths quickened.

Adam looked into those green eyes that captivated him like no other and knew he was lost. She was his—something he'd almost lost out of stupidity and stubbornness.

They came together, calling out each other's names as they did so.

Bay lowered herself so she lay sprawled over his body, his cock still deep within her.

"Why is it that when we do it in a forest, it just seems better?" Bay asked, her voice breathless.

Adam chuckled as he ran a hand down her slick back and cupped her ass, needing to hold her.

"It's better because we can be ourselves wild and free," he finally said.

Bay leaned up, though he still kept a hand on her ass. A man needed touch after all. She tilted her head and bit her lip. "I guess that's true. You don't usually talk about things like that. I like it." She ran her lips across his, and he kissed her slowly, leisurely.

"I'll do it more often," he said once she moved back. "I'll do anything you need."

Just don't leave me.

He didn't say the last part—couldn't say it.

God, she couldn't leave him.

He'd be nothing. Just an empty shell of the man he'd thought he could be.

He'd deserve it.

The crack of thunder brought him out of his thoughts, and fat raindrops started to fall. Bay squealed and lifted herself off him as she laughed.

"Apparently we were too out of it to notice the storm coming," she said as she leaned back to let the rain fall on her face.

"Apparently."

Bay looked down and frowned. "Adam, what were you thinking about before the rain started? You looked so sad."

Damn it.

"Nothing."

"No, don't give me that. You've been looking sad every once in a while for weeks. Just tell me."

"We should change back to our wolves and get home." The

rain increased, soaking their skin as the wind started to pick up.

Bay shook her head, her long red locks sticking to her skin with the rain. "No, not until you tell me."

Adam took a breath. He just needed to get it out. "I was horrible to you."

Bay frowned. "Just now? No, you were amazing."

Hell, he didn't want to have this conversation. He'd rather show her how much he loved her than talk about it. "I meant when we first mated."

Bay's eyes widened. "You had a right. You'd lost your mate and part of your soul."

Adam shook his head. "No, that doesn't give me a right. I treated you like nothing, Bay. How is it that you can forgive me?"

Bay leaned down and framed his face with her hands. "I'm

stronger than you think. I knew fate wouldn't let us down."

Adam met her gaze, needing her to understand. "You shouldn't have had to deal with that."

"I got you out of the deal. I got Micah. What else do I need?"

She didn't understand. "You need more. You need everything. I wish I could go back and tell you I loved you the first moment that I met you and everything I did was because I was lying to myself." Tears ran down his cheeks, mixing with the rain. He didn't need to be the Enforcer right there. He didn't need to be an alpha wolf.

He was only a man who'd hurt his mate.

A man who wasn't *worthy* of his mate.

"I love you, Adam. We can't think about the past. We need to move on."

Adam rested his forehead against hers for a moment before moving back. "I'm going to show you how much I love you with each breath I take because telling you isn't enough."

It would never be enough.

"You already do, by being you," Bay said, and then she kissed him softly.

"That's not good enough for you, Bay. You deserve more."

"I already have it."

He kissed her hard as a weight lifted off his shoulders. He loved this woman, and he'd do whatever he could to show her how much, but that part that had been hurting didn't hurt quite as much anymore.

Who knew he'd just needed the words, the same as she did.

Adam pulled back and tucked a wet piece of hair behind her ear. "Let's change back and go home, my Bay."

FORGIVENESS

Bay nodded, her eyes full of tears, but she looked happy, not sad. That had to mean something.

He loved his mate more than he'd ever thought possible, and maybe, just maybe, he'd feel worthy of her from now on.

CHAPTER 5

Bay stretched her hands over her head, needing to feel free for just a moment before she had to act like a docile wolf in front of the elders. She snorted at the thought.

Sure... her... docile.

In front of the elders, she might be that way, but anyone who knew her knew she wasn't docile in the least. She'd act polite, soothing, and understanding because she had to be and, frankly, because she *wanted* to be.

These wolves had been through everything—wars, famine, death, and a few wonderful happy days in between. She had no idea how old they were—no one really did—but she knew they were older than the Alpha, and some were even older than the den itself.

It was a great honor to be invited into their presence. Most of them were so old and knew so much, but they didn't interact with the den at social functions because the crowds and memories were too much. Even though she knew they would look the same age as her—all adult wolves did—she knew that would be the end of the similarities.

"Ready to go, love?" Adam asked as he walked toward her,

his limp not even noticeable. She was so freaking proud of him for that, though she'd never say it. He knew from the way her eyes crinkled at the corners, but they wouldn't speak of it.

They'd done enough talking about that particular subject.

Ever since their talk in the rain a couple days before, things had changed ever so subtly. It was as if that heavy weight of tension was gone but not forgotten. They didn't change the way they did things, but the stress of doing them had vanished. It was as if they no longer walked on eggshells to prove how much they loved each other.

They just knew.

She smiled at the thought, and Adam pulled her into his arms.

"You taste like brown sugar," he murmured as he licked his way around her lips.

Bay snorted. "It's from our oatmeal this morning. You don't taste so bad yourself."

"Hmm," he purred as he tugged her closer.

She laughed and pulled away. "Oh no you don't, mate of mine. Even though Micah is with Cailin and North today doesn't mean we have free rein to get frisky."

Adam chuckled. "Bay, we *always* have time to get frisky."

Bay rolled her eyes. "Shut it. We're meeting the elders today to talk about the locket. Remember?"

She'd told him about the locket and her vision as soon as they'd gotten home from the forest. He hadn't been hurt that she hadn't told him right away. He'd known that there just hadn't been a right time, not with their work and Micah, but as soon as she told him, he said he'd be by her side the whole way through.

That had warmed her—*still* warmed her.

Reed had set up the appointment for them, and she and Adam would go in front of the elders to show off the locket. She didn't want to hurt anyone with bad memories, but it was as if the locket had told her it *needed* to be found.

Adam gave a little smack to her ass, startling her out of her thoughts even as she warmed from the inside out.

Damn man.

"I'm ready to go if you are," Adam said as he tugged her to the door.

"Do I look okay?" She ran a hand down her sensible green wrap dress. "Does it look slutty?"

Adam rolled his eyes. She loved when he was playful. "You look fine."

She folded her arms over her chest. "Oh no you don't. You

don't get to say I look fine and call it a day. You know that's the man-line for 'I don't care; let's just get out of here.' Do I look slutty?"

Adam laughed. "No, baby, you look great. The green matches your eyes, which you know I love. And the dress doesn't show off your curves to an obscene degree, and your boobs, however sexy they are, aren't falling out. Better?"

She sighed. "I love you. Just thought I'd say that."

"I love you, too. Now let's get going. We don't want to be late."

Panic set in again. "Right. We can't keep them waiting."

Adam took her hand, tangling their fingers, and she settled some. "It's not like meeting the queen, Bay. They're just wolves, older wolves who sometimes look like they know too much, but wolves just the same. You met my dad and acted fine, and he's the Alpha. You'll be okay."

Bay nodded, remembering how scared she'd been meeting Edward when she'd been all alone and heavily pregnant. They hadn't trusted her fully then, but really, she couldn't blame them for that. She'd made it through that, so she should be okay getting though the next part.

Bay took a deep breath as they walked toward the elder homes. They could have driven, but Adam seemed to know she needed the walk and scent of the outdoors to calm her. She was a wolf after all; anything related to nature would ground her.

The six elders lived in a circle of cottages surrounded by tall trees and other greenery, almost hiding them from sight. Their homes were the closest to the den circle where all the Pack meetings and age-old magic took place. Bay still didn't quite understand all that went on within a Pack, but she was learning.

In the center of the property of homes stood a smaller version of the den circle, but it didn't have the stone stadium seating. Rather it had large stone benches around a dirt circle where someone could stand and talk to the elders, almost like being in front of a jury.

Tension crawled its way up her spine and wrapped its hands around her throat. She wasn't ready for this. What if she did something wrong and they banished her? What if the locket held so much pain for its owner that they sent her away?

Adam squeezed her hand then stopped to lean down and kiss her temple. "Calm down, Bay. Your fear is so strong I'm sure any wolf around us can taste it. You'll be fine. You're a

Jamenson. You can't be thrown from the Pack for upsetting someone. You're my mate, my love. You'll always have a home with me."

Relief spread through her at his words. Adam knew exactly what to say to calm her. Thank God she had him and that he understood her more than anyone else—more than anyone *thought* he did.

This was why he didn't need her forgiveness—he already had it.

As they entered the circles of homes, the doors opened and people exited them, heading toward the stone benches in the center. They all looked to be in their mid-thirties, as did the rest of the wolves and the people mated to wolves in the den, but Bay could still sense the power radiating off of them.

FORGIVENESS

It wasn't like the power of the Alpha or any of the Jamensons, which was raw, inherent, and bow-worthy. No, this power tasted of time, wisdom, and memories. Bay couldn't explain it any other way.

These wolves *knew* things.

She held back a shiver. Though knowledge could make them dangerous, she didn't need to feel like prey. Not when she was only there to help and when she had her mate by her side. She'd rather not put him in danger either.

"Hello, Bay Jamenson, and her mate, Adam," the woman directly in front of them said. Her voice sounded of silk, almost wrapping itself around Bay in a warm caress. But Bay felt the raw edge of the silk and knew that voice could lull her into danger...something she'd rather avoid.

"Hello. It's nice to meet you," Bay said.

Hell, she didn't know their names. Was it a sign of disrespect that she didn't? She should have asked Reed or Adam before she came. Too late now.

The woman smiled, and Bay held back a shiver. Yes, this woman was dangerous. Bay really hoped the locket wasn't hers, but rather belonged to one of the other two women by her side, who looked softer. For some reason Bay knew it couldn't have been one of the three men in the circle. No, it had to be one of the women.

"Come," the first woman ordered. "Our Reed said you had something to tell us."

The unearthly way the woman spoke might have creeped her out before, but the possessive tone on Reed's name flat out terrified her for some reason.

Ignoring her thoughts, she and Adam went to the center of the circle and stood, waiting to be told what to do next—not something she enjoyed.

"What is it you wanted to show us?" the woman asked again.

Bay's hands threatened to shake, and she tried to calm herself. She couldn't show weakness, not in front of them. They might not be able to hurt her according to Adam, but they still held power that scared her. She didn't want to mess with them.

Bay took out the locket and held it up. "I found this in the attic of the Alpha and his mate. It resided in the boxes belonging to past elders and wolves, but I wanted to make sure."

She waited for a reaction, but got none.

Okay...

"I don't know if you know about my power—"

"We know of your powers, Bay Jamenson," the woman interrupted.

Bay swallowed hard. "Well, I saw a vision when I held the locket. From that, I had to find its owner so I could give it back. I don't know why, but I felt I had to."

"What was the vision?" the woman asked.

Torn, Bay shook her head. "I want to tell only the owner of the locket." She braced herself for the fallout of that statement. One didn't say no to an elder. Yes, she'd told Reed and Adam about the vision, but Adam was her mate, and Reed helped her find a way to locate the locket's owner. She didn't want to invade the owner's privacy any more than that.

FORGIVENESS

The woman inclined her head, her eyes narrow. "I see."

One of the other women stood and rolled her eyes. "Meryl, shush. You're just nosy." The other woman met Bay's eyes, and Bay froze.

She *knew* those violet eyes. She'd seen them in her vision. Bay hadn't been able to fully see the woman's features in the vision, but she knew those eyes.

The other woman gave a shaky smile. "I'm Emeline, and yes, that is my locket." Emeline swallowed but didn't reach out to take it. "Let's go in my home to talk of this then, shall we?" With that, Emeline turned on her heel and walked toward her home.

Bay looked around at the other elders. Other than Meryl, who stood glaring, sat on their benches, not looking as though they were paying attention, almost as if they were so lost in their own memories that making new ones didn't matter as much.

Bay suppressed a shudder and gave a final nod to them before following Emeline's path. Adam held her hand and squeezed. She looked up at her mate as they walked and fell that much more in love with him.

He'd stood by her side yet let her lead—something that had to be difficult for an alpha wolf. Goddess, he understood her like no other.

She'd have to show how much she appreciated that later. She didn't think making out with him in front of the elders would be appropriate, though they'd probably seen just about everything at this point.

They entered Emeline's home, and Bay held back her surprise. It was bare of mementos and other things that Bay would have thought a woman of

FORGIVENESS

Emeline's experience would have. No, it was as if the woman had been living without *living* or enjoying anything for years.

Bay thought back to the loss and pain she'd felt within the locket and held back a curse. What had this woman done—or, rather, *thought* she'd done?

It seemed Adam wasn't the only one in this room who thought they needed forgiveness. Bay would have to find a way to dig deep and help this woman live again. It had clearly been too long as it was.

Emeline sat on a threadbare couch, her hands clenched in her lap then looked up with tears in her eyes.

"Please, sit." She gestured to the other couch in the room, and Adam and Bay sat, their hands still wrapped around each other's.

"Thank you for inviting us in," Bay said, her voice almost

breaking. The pain in this home was almost unbearable. Something bad had happened, something that had broken the woman in front of her.

Bay squeezed Adam's hand. She knew a little bit about finding the broken, and hoped to God it wasn't what she thought it was.

"May I see the locket?" Emeline asked.

"Of course." Bay held it out to the other woman, but Emeline didn't reach out and take it. Instead her gaze traced it with such longing and pain that Bay wanted to hold the woman in her arms and tell her it would be okay.

"I suppose you want to know about the vision you saw?" The other woman met Bay's gaze as if looking at the locket was too much pain to bear.

"If you'd like to tell us," Bay said. "I don't want you to be upset from it, Emeline. I only brought it here because I felt as though the locket needed to be returned to the one who'd cared for it."

Emeline nodded. "You should know the rest. You see, if you open the locket, you'll see a miniature painting of me...and of my Jeffery." Emeline's voice broke on his name, and Bay reached out and gripped her hand after she put the locket in her pocket.

She didn't care if she'd broken some protocol or taboo. This woman was in so much pain it was thick enough to feel, to taste.

Emeline squeezed back as Adam did the same to Bay's other hand. Together they formed a chain of comfort...and the need to heal.

"Jeffery was my mate." Emeline shook her head, a bitter smile sliding over her face. "No, he *could* have been my mate. My own cowardice prevented that."

Bay didn't say anything, letting the other woman get her story out. Emeline needed to heal.

"It was back in the seventeen hundreds, right when the colonies were declaring their freedom—or at least trying to fight for it. Here in the west, we were just our own settlements, our own Pack, hidden from the humans much more than we are today. The humans didn't come to settle over here until much later, but we let them think they got here first. We didn't fight in that war because it was too far away from us, and frankly I'm not even sure we knew about it. My father was a proud man. Too proud in my opinion." Emeline gave a dry laugh. "In most people's opinions."

Adam rubbed small circles on Bay's wrist, as if knowing she needed the comfort, much like Emeline. Their mate bond flared, settling her.

"My father did not approve of Jeffery," Emeline continued. "Well, that's a minor expression for what he felt for Jeffery. My father hated everything to do with the lesser power and ranking of Jeffery's family. Jeffery himself was stronger than his parents, and their parents before them, but Jeffery was still a submissive wolf."

"Submissive wolves are to be cared for and protected at all costs though," Bay interrupted.

Emeline nodded. "Yes, that's how it *should* be. My father might have felt that way about others—though I don't believe so. It didn't matter what he thought of others though. It only mattered what he thought of the man who would be my mate. My father didn't think Jeffery was good enough for his one and only daughter, so he locked me away."

Tears slid down the other woman's cheeks, and Bay moved to sit by her side and wrapped her arm around Emeline's shoulders. The elder stiffened for a moment before relaxing in Bay's hold. Bay looked up at Adam, who nodded in return, love shining through his eyes.

"Tell us what happened, Emeline," Bay pleaded, knowing the other woman needed to get her story out. It had been far too long.

"You know, Maddox tried to get me to tell this story so often I'm surprised I could hold it back this long," Emeline whispered.

Bay closed her eyes at the thought of the pain Maddox must be sharing. He could feel the emotions in the Pack and would

always be compelled to help—
even those who refused.

"Do you want us to get him?"
Adam asked, breaking his silence.

Bay gave him a grateful look.
If Emeline needed the Omega,
Maddox would be there in a
heartbeat. That was just the kind
of wolf he was.

Emeline shook her head.
"Not yet. Where was I? Oh yes,
being locked away." Emeline
snorted. "That sounds so angst-
filled. He locked me in the
basement and told Jeffery I'd left
the Pack. He said I'd rather run
away and be on my one than be
shackled to a poor man such as
him."

Emeline choked on a sob as
her body shook. "At least, that's
what my father told me. I couldn't
get away, and I tried. Oh, how I
tried, but Jeffery left anyway. You
see, this was back in a time when
the love of a mate had to also help

the Pack and the family. Jeffery didn't see himself as worthy of me because of the way my father looked at him."

Anger filled Bay at the thought. Damn that man for ruining this. Damn that man.

"By the time I escaped, my fingernails gone from digging my way out, it had been too late. Jeffery had left to fight for another Pack, the Talons. They were fighting much like we are now—with the Centrals. He'd left a note saying he was going to prove himself to be worthy of me, even if I didn't want him."

Tears slid down Bay's cheeks as she held Emeline close. "He was already worthy of you," she whispered.

Emeline nodded. "I know this. I *knew* this, but I didn't fight hard enough. I let myself be locked away. I *let* him go and fight."

FORGIVENESS

Bay had a feeling she knew what happened. She'd seen the pain, the loss, and the fire in the vision, but Emeline needed to say it. There had to be a way to purge the guilt and emotions warring within the other woman.

"He died fighting for a Pack that wasn't ours, but a cause just as needy—fighting for a freedom he was denied within his own Pack."

Bay bit her lip so her sobs wouldn't come out and she wouldn't break the fragile hold Emeline had.

"He traveled east to escape my father and prove himself, yet he died in the process. I lost him before I ever had him."

Bay held the woman close as she quietly cried, letting go of centuries of pain and torment.

"I remember this story," Adam said after a while.

Emeline and Bay both looked at Adam, surprise filling her. She hadn't thought that Adam would know any of this, but honestly, she should have. The Jamensons had been around for a while.

"What?" Bay asked.

"My father wasn't Alpha then since his father was still in power, but as the Heir, he heard things. Emeline, you know what happened next, don't you?"

Emeline shook her head. "No, I retreated into myself and didn't pay attention to the Pack for so long. I know my father died, but I don't know why. I didn't care."

Her father was dead? Bay didn't feel any sympathy for that man. No, her sorrow went out to Emeline and Jeffery and the mating bond that had been lost in the process.

Adam sighed. "Your father was a traitor, Emeline. No, he didn't sell out the Pack to another, but he banished a submissive wolf for no reason other than bigotry. My grandfather, the Alpha at the time, fought and killed him in the circle. I didn't realize you didn't know that. In fact, I didn't put two and two together that you were the woman who'd lost everything until you started speaking. I'm so sorry, Emeline."

Emeline stared at Adam with a mixture of pain and hope on her face. "The Pack supported Jeffery? They went against my father?"

Right then, Emeline didn't look like an elder. No, she looked like a young woman who'd lost so much and could maybe, just maybe, live again.

Bay could only hope.

"Yes, Emeline. Your father wasn't the best of men. No, that's being too mild. Your father deserved what he got. You lost something precious to you, Emeline. I know how that feels, believe me."

The pain in his voice was not as pronounced as it had been, and Bay held back a sigh. He'd healed from his loss and now stood with her, ready for their future. She'd shown forgiveness, and her mate was on the path to forgiving himself.

It was Emeline's turn to do the same.

"Emeline," Bay said, "it wasn't your fault. Jeffery died fighting for another Pack and fighting for something he believed in. He wouldn't have wanted you to punish yourself and not live because of it."

Emeline let out a shaky breath. "I...I haven't spoken of him in so long, even if he's been in my heart since then."

"You need to forgive yourself," Bay said, first looking

at Emeline then Adam, knowing they both needed to hear the words.

Adam met her gaze and nodded, and then Emeline turned to Bay. "I'll try," she whispered. "I'll try."

"That's all I ask," Bay said. "That's all anyone can ask. Do you want me to call Maddox now?"

Emeline bit her lip then nodded. "I think it's time."

Relief spread through Bay, and Adam stood to call his brother. Bay took the locket out of her pocket and gently placed it in Emeline's hands.

"Take this," Bay said. "It's yours."

Emeline gripped the locket, her breath shallow. "Thank you. Thank you so much. I threw it into the circle fire when I found out about Jeffery, Edward or his father must have saved it."

Bay nodded then held Emeline close until Maddox came. When the Omega brought Emeline into his arms, whispering soothing words as he was prone to do, Bay left the two quietly talking on the couch, and Adam led her back to their home.

"I think she's going to be okay," Bay said later when they were home with Micah, lying on their bed.

Adam traced her jaw then did the same to Micah, who gripped his finger and smiled. "I think so too. Maddox will help, then Jasper will know who she should talk to. Eventually she might find another mate. I don't think fate thought she was ready for one before, but it might be time."

Bay smiled and rubbed Micah's little tummy. "I hope so. No one deserves to live alone."

Adam cupped her cheek. "Thank you for showing me that."

FORGIVENESS

Bay leaned over Micah to kiss her mate's lips. "You did the same for me, you know. You and Micah, and my wonderful family, are all I need."

Adam had been her salvation, just as she had been his.

No matter what came at them—wars, pain, or strife—they'd have each other.

And that was all she'd ever need.

Coming next in the Redwood Pack World: Shattered Emotions

It's time for Maddox and Ellie to find their peace.

A Note from Carrie Ann

Thank you so much for reading **FORGIVENESS**. I do hope if you liked this story, that you would please leave a review. Not only does a review spread the word to other readers, they let us authors know if you'd like to see more stories like this from us. I love hearing from readers and talking to them when I can. If you want to make sure you know what's coming next from me, you can sign up for my newsletter at www.CarrieAnnRyan.com; follow me on twitter at @CarrieAnnRyan, or like my Facebook page. I also have a Facebook Fan Club where we have trivia, chats, and other goodies. You guys are the reason I get to do what I do and I thank you.

Make sure you're signed up for my MAILING LIST so you can know when the next releases are available as well as find giveaways and FREE READS.

I love going back and visiting characters. Adam and Bay were the hardest couple to write out of the entire Redwood Pack. They crushed me in their need for each other and the obstacles they had to overcome to find their future. This novella was a way to show you what happened once they were a mated couple in truth. Throughout the Redwood Pack series, you will be able to read more after the HEA novellas, so keep an eye out!

I'm also not leaving this world completely. You've met some of the Talons and because I fell for Gideon the first time he walked on the page to help the

Redwoods, I knew I had to tell his story. I also knew I wanted to write some of the Redwood Pack children's stories. Rather than write two full series where I wasn't sure how they would work together, I'm doing one better. The Talon Pack series will be out in early 2015. It is set thirty years in the future and will revolve around the Talon Pack and how they are interacting in the world and with the Redwoods. Because it's set thirty years in the future, I get to write about a few of the Redwood Pack children finding their mates.

The first novel will be about the Talon Alpha Gideon and....Brie, Jasper and Willow's daughter thirty years from now.

If you don't want to wait that long, I also have my Dante's Circle and Montgomery Ink series going in full swing now so there's always a Carrie Ann book on the horizon!

Redwood Pack Series:
Book 1: An Alpha's Path
Book 2: A Taste for a Mate
Book 3: Trinity Bound
Book 3.5: A Night Away
Book 4: Enforcer's Redemption
Book 4.5: Blurred Expectations
Book 4.7: Forgiveness
Book 5: Shattered Emotions
Book 6: Hidden Destiny
Book 6.5: A Beta's Haven
Book 7: Fighting Fate
Book 7.5 Loving the Omega
Book 7.7: The Hunted Heart
Book 8: Wicked Wolf

Want to keep up to date with the next Carrie Ann Ryan Release? Receive Text Alerts easily!
Text CARRIE to 24587

About Carrie Ann and her Books

New York Times and USA Today Bestselling Author Carrie Ann Ryan never thought she'd be a writer. Not really. No, she loved math and science and even went on to graduate school in chemistry. Yes, she read as a kid and devoured teen fiction and Harry Potter, but it wasn't until someone handed her a romance book in her late teens that she realized that there was something out there just for her. When another author suggested she use the voices in her head for good and not evil, The Redwood Pack and all her other stories were born.

Carrie Ann is a bestselling author of over twenty novels and novellas and has so much more on her mind (and on her spreadsheets *grins*) that she isn't planning on giving up her dream anytime soon.

www.CarrieAnnRyan.com

Redwood Pack Series:

The Talon Pack (Following the Redwood Pack Series):
Book 1: Tattered Loyalties
Book 2: An Alpha's Choice
Book 3: Mated in Mist (Coming in 2016)

The Redwood Pack Volumes:
Redwood Pack Vol 1
Redwood Pack Vol 2
Redwood Pack Vol 3
Redwood Pack Vol 4
Redwood Pack Vol 5
Redwood Pack Vol 6

Montgomery Ink:
Book 0.5: Ink Inspired
Book 0.6: Ink Reunited
Book 1: Delicate Ink
Book 1.5 Forever Ink
Book 2: Tempting Boundaries
Book 3: Harder than Words
Book 4: Written in Ink (Coming Oct 2015)

**The Branded Pack Series:
(Written with Alexandra Ivy)**
Books 1 & 2: Stolen and Forgiven
Books 3 & 4: Abandoned and
Unseen (Coming Sept 2015)

Dante's Circle Series:
Book 1: Dust of My Wings
Book 2: Her Warriors' Three
Wishes
Book 3: An Unlucky Moon
The Dante's Circle Box Set
(Contains Books 1-3)
Book 3.5: His Choice
Book 4: Tangled Innocence
Book 5: Fierce Enchantment
Book 6: An Immortal's Song
(Coming in 2016)

Holiday, Montana Series:
Book 1: Charmed Spirits
Book 2: Santa's Executive
Book 3: Finding Abigail
The Holiday Montana Box Set
(Contains Books 1-3)
Book 4: Her Lucky Love

Book 5: Dreams of Ivory

Tempting Signs Series:
Finally Found You

Excerpt: A Beta's Haven

From the next novella in New York Times Bestselling Author Carrie Ann Ryan's Redwood Pack Series

The warm, willing woman in his arms moaned, and Jasper Jamenson pulled her closer, loving the way she arched into him. She was soft, perfect. His. The delicate skin under his hands was familiar, and yet, with each touch, it was like finding something new, something precious, created only for him. His eyes were closed, but he knew he wasn't dreaming, at least he hoped he wasn't. He'd hate to have that happen. Again.

His mate, the love of his life, and his partner, Willow, wiggled her ass against his cock, and he moaned.

Loudly.

"Not so loud, Jasper, you'll wake Brie," Willow whispered, her voice heavy with sleep, gradually filling with need. He felt her body shaking—from holding back laughter or a moan of her own, he wasn't sure. Well, he'd just have to make sure it was the latter. There would be no laughter from his mate while he had his cock pressed against her and when they were both ready to fuck, make love, connect...any of those words that would make them breathe heavy.

He nipped at her neck, and she tilted for him, giving him better access. He licked and sucked at her skin, the salty taste of her body from sleep mixed with the cinnamon that always danced on his tongue when he touched his mouth to her. He'd keep his moans down and try to be quiet, but only because he knew his daughter in the room next to theirs had hearing worthy of any wolf.

"You're the loud one, darling," he teased as he let his hand move to her breast. He plucked at her nipples, loving their reaction to him, pebbling in his palm as he cupped her breasts. He molded them in his hands, taking in their heavy weight. He trailed his hand from between her breasts down over her belly and below the shorts she wore, to the trimmed hair between her legs. He'd never tire of how soft his mate was. Oh, she might not have the full curves of other women, but she was perfect for him.

Willow spread for him, and he circled her clit, his cock

hardening even more at the way she plumped for him with just one easy stroke. He'd make her come on his hand, and then, while she was still cascading down from her high, he'd slide his cock into her heat and pump into her until she came again, and he'd come with her.

Yes, that was a good morning he could live with.

He trailed one finger lower and froze as the door creaked open.

"Daddy! It's breakfast time!" Brie squealed.

Jasper heard her little feet tap against the floor as she ran to his side of the bed. He quickly removed his hand from his wife's pants and rolled to his other side so he could stop Brie from jumping into their bed. With just one look, she came to a stop, sliding a bit before regaining her footing. Jasper had his arm out to catch her, but he wasn't needed.

This time.

"Morning, my baby girl," he said, a smile on his face, even though he hadn't gotten to finish what he'd started with his wife. Again. "What did we say about doors in this house, honey?"

She scrunched up her little face. Her brown hair tumbled in a mess around her head as if she hadn't brushed it in weeks, though he knew Willow had put a braid in it before bed. Brie tended to sleep as wildly as she was when awake. Her braid *never* stayed in place.

His perfect little princess wanted to roughhouse with the boys, and Jasper was fine with it. Sure, she might carry a little more dirt than Willow would like, but at least, this way, Brie would learn to fight off the boys when they came knocking at his perfect little princess's door.

Oh, and when they did, Jasper would be ready.

With his claws.

"Uh, don't open it?"

Jasper rolled his eyes then sat up so he could tickle the little monster beside the bed when she moved closer. She giggled, the high-pitched sound grating on his nerves since he'd just woken up, but at least he knew his daughter was happy. He let her go, and she skipped to the door then looked back.

"Is Mommy making breakfast?" his little girl asked, her eyes dancing.

Willow let out a laugh beside him. He sensed her disappointment that they hadn't finished what they'd started, but mixed with that was her amusement of their daughter, so he reached out and squeezed her hand.

"Yes, Brie dear. Or your daddy can make you cereal if you want."

He looked over at his wife and said, tongue in cheek, "Cereal? That's the best I can do? Is that a comment on my cooking, oh-mate-of-mine?"

Willow blinked up at him with those big hazel eyes he loved, the innocence act so not working.

"I have no idea what you mean, love."

Jasper growled, though he couldn't help the corners of his mouth lifting up. "I didn't poison myself with my own cooking before I met you. I won't poison our daughter."

Willow raised a brow, sitting up to fold her arms under her breasts. "If you could find a way to poison anyone pouring a bowl of cereal, you'd be an extra special Beta, wouldn't you?"

Brie giggled then shifted from side to side. Jasper narrowed his eyes. "Did you use your potty this morning?"

"Maybe," was her reply. She scrunched her face, and he held back a curse.

With the rush of a man who was still learning the steps to this whole father-thing, he picked her up, ran her to her training potty, and let her get to work. She wiggled and smiled as she went about her business, and Jasper just leaned against the sink, wondering how the hell he'd ended up here—a place he loved but was drastically different.

He'd been a bachelor for almost a hundred years, the Beta to the Redwood pack, a Jamenson of royal werewolf blood. Now he was a husband, a mate, a father...and the Beta of a

Pack who was being attacked on an almost daily basis from the Centrals—a Pack now run by a demon from hell rather than a wolf with a bent on ruling the world.

Yes. Things sure seemed to change in the blink of an eye.

And not all for the best.

He wouldn't change who he was and who he'd become for anything in the world. He loved it all. He'd been there when his baby girl was born, even though Willow had kicked him out of the room a few times. He hadn't been able to help it. He and his wolf had wanted to scream at his brother North for taking too long and letting his mate endure so much pain. He'd been there when his baby girl took her first steps, though he'd missed her first words because he'd been out on a call to fulfill his Beta responsibilities.

He'd been able to watch his wife and mate grow and find a rhythm with her wolf, even though the way she'd turned into one of his kind had been brutal and unyielding. He'd been able to watch his brothers fall in love, bond with their mates, and create the next generation of Jamensons.

Through all of that, he'd accepted his responsibility as the Beta, the one wolf who was bonded to the rest of the Pack in such a way that he knew what they needed, sometimes before they did. It was his job to ensure the needs of the Pack were taken care of so the others around him could function and move forward.

He loved his role in the Pack—even if he was so tired some nights the effort it took to breathe was almost too much.

With the Pack on the defense most days with battles and the

threat of war, the health—emotional, physical, and functional—of their members needed to remain high, even if it wasn't necessarily Jasper's job to ensure it. Both he and his wolf knew when a Pack member needed something, such as time off or to focus on a new project, but that didn't mean Jasper had to hold their hand to make it happen.

He did it because he wanted to.

Maddox, his twin brother, was the Omega, so he helped with emotional health of the Pack, much like Hannah, his sister-in-law, the Healer, helped with their physical health.

Jasper was the jack of all trades, doing what the moon goddess needed, even if he didn't have a clear daily job these days. Between war meetings with the family, actual battles with the

Centrals, and his duties as Beta, he didn't spend as much time with Willow and Brie as he wanted to, and that hurt above all else. He could deal with the lack of sleep and barely scraping by his responsibilities, but he was missing so much with his family, and in that, he knew something had to change.

He just had no idea what.

If only the Beta could have an assistant or something.

"Daddy, I'm done."

Jasper blinked and looked down at his little girl, who smiled up at him. He helped her wash her hands, took care of her training potty, washed his own hands twice more, and then carried Brie out of the bathroom upside down. He could have held her correctly, but he loved the way she squealed. He dodged a stray kick to the chin and kept moving.

As he moved, he caught a newer scent coming from his baby girl, one that had more to do with the magic within her ready to burst free than anything she might have rolled in. Knowing Brie, she could have rolled in just about anything.

His wolf nudged up against him, and he smiled. Yes, his little girl would be doing her shift soon. His own wolf could tell. All werewolves were born human, and usually, between the ages of two and three, they made their first shift into wolf pups. At that age, they had a little more control over their bodies to make the change, though all pups were a little rambunctious.

"Down, Daddy, down!" Brie giggled, the high-pitched sound not as grating now that he was awake, but damn, he needed coffee.

He set her down on her feet, and she scrambled to her chair in the dining room. Jasper followed his nose to the scent of fresh coffee then leaned against the archway so he could watch Willow in her element. No, he wasn't being a chauvinistic ass. His Willow loved cooking and was freaking amazing at it. He still remembered the taste of the first omelet she'd made for him in this house and how he'd wanted to kneel at her feet and ask her to stay forever.

Okay, he might have done that anyway because his love and need for her wasn't only for her omelets.

He licked his lips at the scent of the cinnamon from the rolls in the air blending with the sugar and cinnamon from his mate's skin. He and his wolf loved the fact that his mate carried the scent of her famous cinnamon rolls on her skin.

Yep, she was totally perfect for him.

He came up from behind her and pulled her close. She laid her head back and sighed. "I'm almost done, then the rolls will have to bake for twenty minutes. I know Brie is hungry now, but I was in the mood for something extra sweet."

He nibbled at her neck and hummed against her. "Me too, love."

Willow laughed and wiggled away, the motion only making his cock stand more at attention. "Shoo. Go get Brie her yogurt so she at least has something nutritious. She can have half a roll when they're done."

He did as he was told and sat next to his daughter as she ate, laughing and telling him a story about her cousin Finn and how he'd turned into his wolf then tried to climb on a picnic table but had forgotten he had four paws instead of two feet.

He leaned back, sipping on his coffee, trying to ignore the long list of items he needed to get through and just listened to his daughter ramble. When she finished her story and ate more of her yogurt, she danced in her seat, unable to keep still for even a moment.

Jasper ran a hand through his hair, noticing it was again reaching his shoulders. His mother would scold him in that sweet way of hers, but Willow seemed to like it. Still, he needed to start taking better care of himself.

"Hey, Willow, what do you say the three of us go for a picnic or something today?"

Willow came out of the kitchen to the dining room, a

frown on her face as she dried her hands. "Don't you have to go to Isaiah's house today then Ms. Clerk's? They need your help with fixing something or other. After that, you have that meeting with Adam about patrols. You have to make sure that people are getting their shifts worked out, so they have a breather like they should, even though I think Adam knows that already."

Jasper shook his head and stood up so he could bring her closer. "I think everyone can handle a day without me. Right?" Before the war, before he'd had his family, he'd been able to do just that. Now, though, things were different.

Willow smiled, her eyes bright. "I'd love it if you could do that. I have people coming into the bakery today to work. I was planning on taking the day off to play with Brie anyway. We'd love it if you could come with us."

He grinned, his body relaxing for the first time in too long. He brought his lips to hers and sank against his mate.

His cell phone rang on the counter, and he cursed. "Let's hope that's something I can ignore."

Willow gave a sad smile, patted his cheek, and then shook her head. "I know you love your job as Beta, Jasper. No, that's not right... It's not a job; it's your calling, your duty. Do what you need to. Brie and I will be here. I promise."

He kissed her forehead then picked up his cell. Of course it wasn't something he could ignore, as it was one of the newly widowed witches in the Pack, Calista, who'd lost her husband during one of the Centrals' attacks. Emotionally, she was a wreck, but she was maintaining with Maddox's help. Jasper also had a duty to her, to be there to make sure she had all she needed to raise her kids, live her life, and try to find a way to move on.

After dressing for the day, and following a regretful kiss goodbye to his girls, he made his way to Calista's. She was in a rare position in that she didn't have any family within the den to help with things like a leaky pipe in her basement—the current job Jasper had to help with. Yes, his actual job in the human world, when he could get to it, was a contractor, but he barely remembered that world these days. Calista, however, didn't have a job in the human realm. She'd been a stay-at-home wife to her mate and mom to her six children, something she loved.

Mateo, her late husband, had been one of the Alpha's enforcers, a bodyguard to the Alpha, and had died protecting the Pack on patrol. Now Calista was alone, with no family except for Mateo's great aunt who, at four hundred and twelve, was long past the age of wanting to help raise kids. She did it though. Calista wasn't alone and was a strong enough woman that her kids were in a better place than they would have been if she hadn't had such a steely backbone.

The woman couldn't fix a leaky pipe though—something that pissed her off.

"I don't understand it, Jasper," she said as she soothed her four-year-old and brushed her six-year-old's hair at the same time. "If it was just a normal leak, I could fix it, but this? This looks big."

Well, she wasn't wrong. The woman's basement currently resembled a small lake. Since

Calista wasn't a wolf and didn't have those extra senses, she hadn't been able to hear the room filling with water. She'd caught it before it had gotten any worse only because one of her kids had noticed it.

"You could call it that," Jasper answered easily. "I'm going to have to call Kade or someone else in to help me fix it."

Calista sighed but nodded. "Is there something special I need to know about for cleanup?"

"Yeah, but I'll bring people over to help. You've got enough on your plate to worry about mold."

"Oh goddess. Mold?" Her voice rose to a squeak, and Jasper winced.

"We'll take care of it. Don't you worry." He ran a hand over one of the little girls' hair, missing his own Brie.

"I don't know what I'd do without you, Jasper. I don't know what the Pack would do you without you. You're a great Beta."

Jasper gave a tight smile and got to work. Yes, he might have been a great Beta, but he was a fucking tired one. He'd wanted to spend time with his girls, and now he was knee-deep in murky water.

Oh, the joys of duty and fate.

He loved his job, he really did. He just wanted to go back to a time when he had something else...something that was just about him.

Something gurgled behind him, and he turned, only to find himself drenched and dripping with sewage.

Fuck it.

He looked down at what he hoped was mud on his shirt.

He needed a vacation.

Or at least a towel.

Jasper let out a breath then bent to pick up his tool box from the steps. Seeing how he was mired in his own head and not paying attention like he should have been, he didn't see the rusty pipe sticking out of the wall.

His head slammed into it, and he saw stars, swallowing back bile as he fell to his knees, the water now up to his chest.

He blinked a couple times, and then, just as the darkness slid over him, he heard shouts and his name.

At least he wouldn't drown alone. He definitely needed a break.

Dust of My Wings

From New York Times Bestselling Author Carrie Ann Ryan's Dante's Circle Series

Humans aren't as alone as they choose to believe. Every human possesses a trait of supernatural that lays dormant within their genetic make-up. Centuries of diluting and breeding have allowed humans to think they are alone and untouched by magic. But what happens when something changes?

Neat freak lab tech, Lily Banner lives her life as any ordinary human. She's dedicated to her work and loves to hang out with her friends at Dante's Circle, their local bar. When she discovers a strange blue dust at work she meets a handsome stranger holding secrets – and maybe her heart. But after a close call with a thunderstorm, she may not be as ordinary as she thinks.

Shade Griffin is a warrior angel sent to Earth to protect the supernaturals' secrets. One problem, he can't stop leaving dust in odd places around town. Now he has to find every ounce of his dust and keep the presence of the supernatural a secret. But after a close encounter with a sexy lab tech and a lightning quick connection, his millennia old loyalties may shift and he could lose more than just his wings in the chaos.

Warning: Contains a sexy angel with a choice to make and a green-eyed lab tech who dreams of a dark-winged stranger. Oh yeah, and a shocking spark that's sure to leave them begging for more.

Ink Inspired

From New York Times Bestselling Author Carrie Ann Ryan's Montgomery Ink Series

Shepard Montgomery loves the feel of a needle in his hands, the ink that he lays on another, and the thrill he gets when his art is finished, appreciated, and loved. At least that's the way it used to be. Now he's struggling to figure out why he's a tattoo artist at all as he wades through the college frat boys and tourists who just want a thrill, not a permanent reminder of their trip. Once he sees the Ice Princess walk through Midnight Ink's doors though, he knows he might just have found the inspiration he needs.

Shea Little has spent her life listening to her family's desires. She went to the best schools, participated in the most proper of social events, and almost married the man her family wanted for her. When she ran from that and found a job she actually likes, she thought she'd rebelled enough. Now though, she wants one more thing—only Shepard stands in the way. She'll not only have to let him learn more about her in order to get inked, but find out what it means to be truly free.

Printed in Great Britain
by Amazon

35548957R00097